MW01100814

A Note to Parents and Caregivers:

Read-it! Joke Books are for children who are moving ahead on the amazing road to reading. These fun books support the acquisition and extension of reading skills as well as a love of books.

Published by the same company that produces *Read-it!* Readers, these books introduce the question/answer pattern that helps children expand their thinking about language structure and book formats.

When sharing a book with your child, read in short stretches, pausing often to talk about the pictures and the meaning of the book. The question/answer format works well for this purpose and provides an opportunity to talk about the language and meaning of the jokes. Have your child turn the pages and point to the pictures and familiar words. Read the story in a natural voice; have fun creating the voices of characters or emphasizing some important words. And be sure to reread favorite parts.

There is no right or wrong way to share books with children. Find time to read with your child, and pass on the legacy of literacy.

Adria F. Klein, Ph.D.
Professor Emeritus
California State University
San Bernardino, California

Managing Editor: Bob Temple

Creative Director: Terri Foley

Editor: Sara E. Hoffmann

Designers: John Moldstad, Amy Bailey

Page production: Picture Window Books

The illustrations in this book were prepared digitally.

Picture Window Books

5115 Excelsior Boulevard

Suite 232

Minneapolis, MN 55416

1-877-845-8392

www.picturewindowbooks.com

Printed in the United States of America.

Library of Congress Cataloging-in-Publication Data

Dahl, Michael.

Crazy criss-cross : a book of mixed-up riddles / written by Michael Dahl ; illustrated by Garry Nichols.

p. cm. — (Read-it! joke books)

Summary: A collection of riddles that begin "What do you get when you cross..."

ISBN 1-4048-0232-0

1. Riddles, Juvenile. 2. Riddles.

I. Nichols, Garry, ill. II. Title.

PN6371.5 .D33 2004

818'.602—dc21

2003014345

Crazy
Criss-Cross

A Book of Mixed-Up Riddles

Michael Dahl • Illustrated by Garry Nichols

Reading Advisers:
Adria F. Klein, Ph.D.
Professor Emeritus, California State University
San Bernardino, California

Susan Kesselring, M.A., Literacy Educator
Rosemount-Apple Valley-Eagan (Minnesota) School District

PICTURE WINDOW BOOKS
Minneapolis, Minnesota

What do you get when you cross your grandmother with a flock of ducks?

Gram-quackers.

What do you get when you cross a pig with an evergreen tree?

A porky-pine.

What do you get when you cross a ghost with an Italian restaurant?

Spooketti.

What do you get when you cross a baby with a basketball player?

Lots of dribbling.

What do you get when you cross a cowboy with an octopus?

Billy the Squid.

What do you get when you cross a cheetah with a cheeseburger?

Fast food.

What do you get when you cross a stick of gum with a railroad track?

A chew-chew train.

What do you get when you cross a spider with a field of corn?

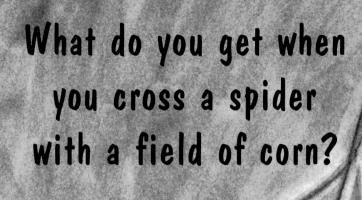

Cob webs.

What do you get when you cross an elephant with a fish?

Swimming trunks.

What do you get when you cross a bread truck with a dragon?

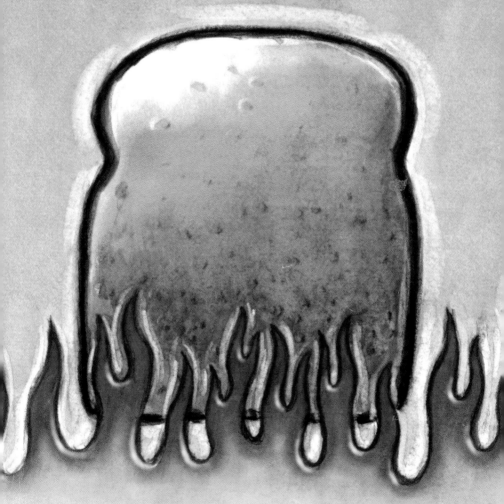

Toast.

What do you get when
you cross a burglar
with a surfboard?

A crime wave.

What do you get when you cross a pig with a karate teacher?

Pork chops.

What do you get when
you cross a mouth
with a tornado?

A tongue twister.

What do you get when you cross a bunch of grapes with a busy street?

Traffic jam.

What do you get when you cross a ghost with a television set?

A big-scream TV.

21

What do you get when you cross a reptile with a telephone?

A croc-o-dial.

What do you get when you cross a snowman with a vampire?

Frostbite.